It Can't Be

Andrew David Hewitt

authorHOUSE®

AuthorHouse™
1663 Liberty Drive
Bloomington, IN 47403
www.authorhouse.com
Phone: 1-800-839-8640

First published by AuthorHouse   01/12/2012

ISBN: 978-1-4678-8329-0 (sc)
ISBN: 978-1-4678-8330-6 (ebk)

Printed in the United States of America

CONTENTS

O N March 17, 1960, the administration of US President Dwight D. Eisenhower agreed to a recommendation from the Central Intelligence Agency to equip and train Cuban exiles for action against the new Cuban government of Fidel Castro.

Eisenhower stated it was the policy of the US government to aid anti-Castro guerrilla forces; the CIA was initially confident it was capable of overthrowing the Cuban government, having experience assisting in the overthrow of the governments of Iranian Prime Minister Mohammed Mossadegh in 1953 and Guatemalan President Jacobo Arbenz Guzman in 1954.

The original plan called for landing invasion ground forces in the vicinity of the old colonial city of Trinidad, Cuba, in the central province of Sancti Spiritus, approximately 400 kilometres (250 miles) south-east of Havana, at the foothills of the Escambray Mountains The Trinidad site provided several options that the ground forces could exploit during the invasion.

The CIA began to recruit and train anti-Castro forces in the Sierra Madres on the Pacific coast of Guatemala. These forces were named Brigade 2506 (*Brigada Asalto* 2506), and the overall plan was code-named Operation Zapata (aka Operation Pluto) by the CIA.

CIA director Allen Dulles appointed one of his aides, Richard Mervin Bissell Jr., as director of Operation Zapata.

As the plans evolved, critical aspects were changed, including the location of the landing area for Brigade 2506 to two points in Matanzas Province, 200 kilometres south-east of Havana on the eastern edge of the Zapata peninsula at the Bay of Pigs. The landings would take place on the Giron and Zapatos Larga beaches (code-named Blue Beach and Red Beach, respectively). This change effectively cut off contact with the rebels of the "war against the bandits" uprising in the Escambray Mountains.

WARNINGS

T HE CUBAN SECURITY APPARATUS knew the invasion was coming, via their secret intelligence network, as well as loose talk by members of the brigade, some of which was heard in Miami and was repeated in US and foreign newspaper reports.

Nevertheless, days before the invasion, multiple acts of sabotage were carried out, such as the bombing of the El Enchanto Department Store in Havana, desultory explosions, and arson.

The Cuban government also had been warned by senior KGB agents Osvaldo Sanchez Cabrera and "Aragon," who both died violently before and after the invasion, respectively.

The Cuban population was not well informed, except for Radio Swan, the anti-Castro pirate radio station funded by the CIA.

As of May 1961, almost all of public communication was in government hands.

Personages Involved

S OVIET-TRAINED ADVISORS WERE BROUGHT to Cuba from the eastern bloc countries. These advisors had held high positions in the Soviet army during World War II and resided in the Soviet Union for long periods, thus they were known as "Hispano-Soviets."

The most senior of these were the Spanish Communists of the Spanish civil war: Francisco Ciutat de Miguel, Enrique Lister, and Alberto Bayo. Ciutat de Miguel's Russian name was Pavel Pavlovich Stepanov, and his Cuban alias was Angel Martinez Riosola (commonly referred to as Angelito), who is said to have arrived the same day as the La Coubre Explosion; he was wounded in the foot during the war against the bandits.

The role of other Soviet agents at the time is not well known, although they were well established in Cuba at the time of the Bay of Pigs invasion, and it can be presumed that they were actively involved in the Cuban government's defence.

SUPPRESSION

N O QUARTER WAS GIVEN during the attack in the Escambray Mountains, where former rebels from the War against Batista took different sides.

Potential enemies of the revolution were neutralized, arrested, or shot while resisting arrest. Because of the lack of prison space, suspected counter-revolutionaries were unceremoniously rounded up and corralled in any facility available, be it sports stadium, school, or school yard, to prevent the people from aiding the expected invading force.

By the time the invasion began, Cuban government authorities had already executed some who were suspected of colluding with the American campaign; however, the CIA seemed blissfully unaware of the effects of this repression on the planned operation.

Notably, two former "comandantes," Humberto Sori Marin and William Alexander Morgan, and others were executed, included Alberto Tapia Ruano, a Catholic youth leader. Several hundred thousand people were imprisoned before, during, and after the invasion.

Invasion day was on April 17, 1961. Four 2,400-ton chartered ships (the *Houston, Rio Escondido, Caribe, Atlantico*) transported 1,511 Cuban exiles to the Bay of Pigs on the southern coast of Cuba. They were accompanied by two CIA-owned infantry landing craft (LCIs) called *Blager* and *Barbara J*, containing supplies, ordnance, and equipment. The group was also known as the Cuban expeditionary force. The small contingent hoped to find support from the local population and intended to cross the island to Havana. The CIA assumed the invasion would spark a popular uprising against the Cuban government of Fidel Castro; however, the Escambray rebels had been contained by Cuban militia directed by Francisco Ciutat de Miguel.

In the beginning, the Cuban militia on the beach surrendered, and the invaders moved to control the causeways across the Zapata swamps. There the fighting became intense, and the Cuban militia and army casualties were high, as a result of firepower from both Brigade 2506 and B-26 aircraft. After landing, it soon became evident that the Brigade 2506 ground forces were not going to receive effective support at the site of the invasion and were likely to lose. After the initial success, the CIA/Brigade 2506 forces suffered considerable reverses.

Kennedy decided against giving the faltering invasion US air support because of his opposition to overt intervention. Kennedy had also cancelled sorties of attacks on Cuban airfields planned for April 16 and 17.

AFTERMATH CASUALTIES

AIRCREWS KILLED IN ACTION between April 15 and 19 totalled six from Cuban air forces, ten Cuban exiles, and four citizens by the time fighting ended on April 21. Sixty-eight brigade ground forces were killed in action, and the rest were captured.

The Cuban losses during the invasion are unknown but most sources estimate them to be in the thousands. Unofficial reports list that seven Cuban army infantry battalions suffered significant losses during the fighting. The Cuban government initially reported its army losses to be eighty-seven dead and many more wounded during the days of fighting the invaders. The number of those killed in action in Cuba's army during the battle eventually ran to 140, and then finally to 161. However, these figures are for Cuban army losses only, not militia or armed civilian loyalists. Thus, in the most accepted calculations, a total of around 2,000 (perhaps as many as 5,000) Cuban militia fighting for the Republic of Cuba may have been killed, wounded, or missing in action.

PRISONERS

T HE 1,209 CAPTURED MEMBERS of Brigade 2506 were quickly put on trial for treason; a few were executed, and the rest were sentenced to thirty years in prison. On April 21, 1961, at least seven Cubans plus two US civilians (Angus K. McNair and Howard F. Anderson) were executed in Pinar del Rio Province.

In May 1961, Fidel Castro proposed an exchange of the surviving members of the assault for 500 large tractors, presumably for agriculture; the trade rose to US$28 million; negotiations were nonproductive until after the Cuban missile crisis. On December 21, 1962, Castro and James B. Donovan, a US lawyer, signed an agreement to exchange the 1,113 prisoners for US$53 million in food and medicine; the money was raised by private donations. On December 29, 1962, Kennedy met with returning brigade members at Palm Beach, Florida.

Between April and October 1961, hundreds of executions took place at various prisons, particularly at the dreaded Fortaleza de la Cabana and El Morro Castle, the eighteenth-century Spanish fortresses that protected Havana Harbour. The government authorities had converted their dungeons into prisons, their walls into firing squad walls. Team leaders Antonio Diaz Pou and Raimundo E. Lopez, as well as underground students Virgilio Campaneria, Alberto Tapia, and more than a hundred others died within these colonial prisons.

REACTION

THE FAILED INVASION SEVERELY embarrassed the Kennedy administration and made Castro wary of future intervention in Cuba. As a result of the failure, CIA Director Allen Dulles, Deputy CIA Director Charles Cabell, and Deputy Director of Operations Richard Bissell all resigned. All three were held responsible for the planning of the operation at the CIA. Responsibility of the Kennedy administration and the US State Department for the modifications of the plans were not apparent until later.

CUBAN MISSILE CRISIS

HIS WAS A MAJOR confrontation during the cold war between the United States and the Union of Soviet Socialist Republics (USSR) that occurred in 1962 over the issue of Soviet-supplied missile installations in Cuba. Regarded by many as the closest the world has approached nuclear war, the crisis began when the United States discovered that Cuba had secretly installed Soviet missiles able to carry nuclear weapons. These missiles were capable of hitting targets across most of the United States. The discovery led to a tense standoff over several days as the United States imposed a naval blockade of Cuba and demanded that the USSR remove the missiles.

The crisis was the culmination of growing tension between the United States and Cuba following the Cuban revolution of 1959. The revolution ousted Cuba's US-backed dictator, Fulgencio Batista, and brought to power a government headed by the revolutionary leader Fidel Castro.

Prior to the revolution, the United States had had significant influence in Cuba's economic and political affairs, but the Castro government resisted the hegemony of the United States. Castro also caused concern in the United States when he confiscated property belonging to wealthy Cubans and foreigners in an attempt to implement policies to improve conditions for poor and working-class Cubans. Many of these properties belonged to businesses owned by US companies.

Fearing that Castro would establish a Communist regime in Cuba, the United States applied economic pressure, and in 1960 implemented an embargo that cut off trade with Cuba. Castro responded by establishing closer relations with the Communist government of the USSR.

CRISIS EMERGES

I N 1960, AS TENSIONS mounted between Cuba and the United States, Soviet Premier Nikita Khrushchev began planning to secretly supply Cuba with missiles that could deliver nuclear warheads to most parts of the United States.

Khrushchev mistakenly assumed that the United States would take no action.

By 1962, however, concern was growing in the United States over reports that the USSR was channelling weapons to Cuba.

In September, US President John Fitzgerald Kennedy warned the Soviets that "the gravest issues" would ensue should they place offensive weapons (a phrase widely understood to mean nuclear weapons) in Cuba.

On October 14, US spy planes flying over Cuba spotted the first ballistic missiles. On October 16, intelligence officials presented Kennedy with photographs showing nuclear missile bases under construction in Cuba. The photos suggested preparations for two types of missiles: medium-range ballistic missiles (MRBMs) able to travel about 1,100 nautical miles (about 2,000 kilometres, or 1,300 miles) and intermediate-range ballistic missiles (IRBMs) able to reach targets at a distance of about 2,200 nautical miles (about 4,100 kilometres or 2,500 miles). These missiles placed most US cities—including Los Angeles, Chicago, and New York—within range of nuclear attack. Kennedy also saw evidence of nuclear-capable bombers.

Kennedy now faced a situation with potentially grave consequences. However, he had no clear choice on the actions to take against the Cubans and Soviets. He knew that an attack on Soviet installations in Cuba risked touching off a global nuclear war that would result in the loss of millions of lives. At the same time, he thought, and repeatedly said, that he also risked war by doing nothing. If he ignored Soviet defiance on his pledge in September to oppose offensive weapons in Cuba, then all US pledges might become suspect.

A US promise to defend West Berlin was already under severe pressure. Earlier in the year, Khrushchev had threatened to take over West Berlin and told Kennedy he was willing to bring the matter to the point of war. Khrushchev set a deadline of November 1962 for the resolution of the issue. Before the Cuban missile crisis began, Kennedy and his advisers believed US nuclear superiority would deter any aggressive Soviet moves. But when the photos of the missiles arrived, Kennedy and his experts agreed that the weapons might have been placed in Cuba to keep the United States from going to war over West Berlin. For Kennedy, doing nothing about the missiles would only increase the danger in another war, threatening a crisis later in the year, this time over Berlin.

The dilemma, as Kennedy understood it, was acute.

THE OPTIONS

KENNEDY QUICKLY ASSEMBLED A small circle of advisers, including both national security officials and others whose judgement Kennedy valued. On October 16, the first day of the crisis, Kennedy and many of his advisers agreed that a surprise air attack against Cuba, followed by a blockade and an invasion, might be the only effective response to the threat posed by the Soviet missiles.

On October 18, however, former US ambassador to the Soviet Union, Llewellyn Thompson, suggested that Kennedy announce a blockade as a prelude to an air strike. Kennedy's advisers supported a blockade, but not all for the same reasons. One group saw the blockade as a form of ultimatum. Unless Khrushchev announced he would pull the missiles out of Cuba, the blockade would be very shortly followed by some form of military action. Another group saw the blockade as an opening to negotiation. After his advisers debated the options, Kennedy decided to go ahead with the blockade. At the same time, the US military began moving soldiers and equipment into position for a possible invasion of Cuba.

Before Kennedy publicly announced the blockade, he wanted to prepare both military and congressional leaders. On October 19, he met with the Joint Chiefs of Staff, and he met with congressional leaders on October 22. Following these meetings, Kennedy went on radio and television and announced the discovery of the missiles. He demanded that Khrushchev withdraw them and said that as a first step, he was initiating a naval quarantine zone around Cuba, within which US naval forces would intercept and inspect ships to determine whether they were carrying weapons. Kennedy warned that if Khrushchev fired missiles from Cuba, the result would be "a full retaliatory response on the Soviet Union." Because international law defines a blockade as an act of war, Kennedy and his advisers decided to refer to the blockade as a quarantine.

WAITING FOR WAR

THE FIRST DAYS AFTER the speech were consumed with tension as Kennedy waited to see whether the Soviet ships would respect the blockade or trigger a military confrontation at sea. For several tense days, Soviet vessels en route to Cuba avoided the quarantine zone, and Kennedy and Khrushchev communicated through diplomatic channels. This cautious action postponed any confrontation between the US Navy and the Soviet freighters and the Soviet submarines escorting them.

On October 26, Khrushchev sent a coded cable to Kennedy that seemingly offered to withdraw missiles from Cuba in return for a US pledge not to invade the island, a pledge Kennedy had volunteered more than a week earlier during a meeting with Soviet Foreign Minister Andrei Gromyko. Before Kennedy and his advisers could react, Khrushchev delivered a public message in which he linked the withdrawal of the Cuban missiles to the removal of "analogous" US weapons in Turkey (a member of NATO), along the southern border of the USSR. Khrushchev may have been emboldened to make this added demand by the fact that the United States allowed some Soviet bloc ships to pass through the blockade. None of Kennedy's advisers valued the missiles in Turkey, which were considered obsolete. However, nearly all of them counselled against removing them in response to the Soviet demand, a demand they thought was made in bad faith to derail any solution.

Meanwhile, the United States faced the difficult problems of maintaining the blockade and keeping track of the Soviet missiles, which were camouflaged and moved soon after Kennedy's speech. Low flying US surveillance aircraft encountered hostile fire, and on October 27, the Cubans shot down a U-2 spy plane, killing its pilot. The Kennedy administration debated the question of whether or not to retaliate by destroying some air defence installations in Cuba, but retaliation ran the risk of killing Soviet military advisers and thereby escalating the crisis.

Kennedy sensed that the US public would accept the removal of the missiles in Turkey, but he did not want to appear to be capitulating to Khrushchev's demand. Finally Kennedy decided his public reply would only address Khrushchev's first message, which had offered to withdraw the missiles in exchange for a pledge not to invade Cuba.

At the same time, however, Kennedy planned to privately assure Khrushchev that he intended to remove the missiles in Turkey. The president's brother, Attorney General Robert Kennedy, paid a secret visit to Soviet Ambassador Anatoly Dobrynin at the Soviet embassy in Washington DC, to convey the president's pledge and its terms. If the Soviets disclosed the assurance or intimated that the missiles in Turkey were part of the bargain, the missiles would not be withdrawn, Robert Kennedy told Dobrynin. He also warned the Soviets that time was running out and that the president would soon feel compelled to attack Cuba.

By the time he received Dobrynin's report, however, Khrushchev had already decided to remove the missiles because the danger of nuclear war was too great. Castro had sent Khrushchev a message saying that he believed a US invasion was imminent and that Khrushchev should be ready to launch the missiles. Khrushchev decided that Kennedy was serious and that an air attack on Cuba and an invasion were at hand. Khrushchev told his ministers that the missiles must be withdrawn from Cuba in return for a noninvasion pledge.

RESOLUTION

O N OCTOBER 28, THE tension began to subside; in a radio broadcast, Khrushchev said he would remove "offensive" weapons from Cuba in return for a US pledge not to invade. He also called for UN inspectors to verify the process. Kennedy believed Khrushchev was sincere, but many of Kennedy's advisers remained wary of Soviet intentions.

A further problem developed when Castro refused to allow UN oversight of the dismantling process. Eventually an agreement was reached; the bombers would be removed in thirty days, and the missiles and other "offensive "weapons would be evacuated in the open so that US surveillance aircraft could observe their removal.

CONCLUSION

I N THE YEARS SINCE the crisis, more details about the incident emerged from declassified US and Soviet files; from interviews involving those who participated in the crisis, including some Soviet officials; and from the release of secretly recorded White House tapes of the meetings involving Kennedy and his advisers. The facts that came to light revealed that a US invasion of Cuba might have met more opposition than the United States expected; unknown to the US government, Soviet forces in Cuba had been equipped with nuclear weapons intended for battlefield use. The United States had also incorrectly estimated the number of Soviet troops stationed in Cuba. Any US invasion would have faced stiff resistance.

The crisis led to a temporary strain in relations between the USSR and Cuba. Castro felt he had been unfairly excluded from the negotiations over the fate of the missiles, which he thought Cuba needed to discourage a potential invasion from the United States. However, with the threat of invasion removed by the US pledge and with Cuba badly in need of Soviet financial aid, relations soon grew closer.

The apparent capitulation of the USSR in the standoff was instrumental in Khrushchev's removal as leader of the USSR in 1964. The younger Soviet leaders who ousted Khrushchev perceived his actions during the crisis as weak and indecisive. The Cuban missile crisis also marked the point at which the cold war began to "thaw."

Khrushchev eventually accepted the status quo in West Berlin, and the predicted conflict there never materialized. The thaw also led to the signing of the Limited Nuclear Test Ban Treaty in 1963 by the United Kingdom, the United States, and the USSR, which outlawed test explosions in the atmosphere or underwater.

The Cuban missile crisis was a very dangerous episode, bringing the world's major military powers to the brink of nuclear war. Kennedy had been criticized for such policies as the failed Bay of Pigs invasion, which helped cement the Soviet-Cuban relationship and led Khrushchev to think Kennedy might be bullied. Yet most historians agree that it was Kennedy's good judgement, and the prudence Khrushchev displayed once the crisis intensified, that helped avert catastrophe.

CHAPTER 1

O N FRIDAY, NOVEMBER 20, in England, a ch-47 Chinook military transport helicopter circled over Sandhurst Military Training College, situated on the A30 between Basingstoke and Bagshot.

The Chinook hovered above the massive lawn in front of the main building; you know the type, the one where all the regimental dinners are held. It's a lovely, massive white building (I'd hate to guess how many windows it has).

Out of this building, a man in a very expensive suit appeared. He walked tall and straight; this man is Major General Rutherford Jones.

He is the commandant of the academy, the main man. He was there to meet the helicopter, whose arrival was a secret, one that must be kept at all cost.

The ch-47 Chinook moved in and landed. The people inside waited for the blades to stop, and when the door slid open, out stepped a man in his mid-forties. He was a good looking man about six feet tall with dark hair and a tan.

He walked over to the major general and they shook hands. The major general told him that all the arrangements had been made.

The man from the copter said, "I can rely on your total discretion and privacy while we are here."

The major general assured him of this and said, "I guarantee it."

The man thanked him and said it was imperative they have privacy.

At this point, he turned around and signalled to the Chinook. Two men appeared and climbed out; they looked like Secret Service men, or maybe CIA. Both were over six feet tall, with black suits and chiselled features, no smiles allowed, and the compulsory dark glasses and earpieces.

Then a man in a wheelchair was brought to the door by an older woman; she looked to be in her mid-eighties, but you could tell she used to be a looker in her day. The man was also in his eighties. The two men moved to the copter and grabbed the wheelchair and lifted the man down.

The major general said, "Please follow me and I'll show you to your accommodations."

The first man thanked him and they followed the major general. He led them in front of the main building, and then they turned to the right towards the specially prepared summer house. This was where the major general's guests stayed when visiting. He led them to the door but didn't show them inside; he wished them all the best and told them if they needed anything, he would get it for them.

The first man thanked him, and the major general walked away. The visitors entered the house; in one of the bedrooms, there was an hospital bed and breathing equipment; there were also two other single bedrooms, a bathroom, a kitchen, and a TV-dining room. The agents wheeled the old man into the bedroom, and the other people followed. The old woman pulled back the bed sheets, and the two agents gently lifted the man into the bed. The lady put a pillow behind his shoulders and neck to make him comfy.

She said, "Rest now, darling. I'll be back soon." She left the room and went to the young man's room and helped him unpack, as the two agents stood guard outside.

As the major general walked home, he bumped into his wife, who was taking their chocolate Labrador for a walk.

"Hello, love," she said. "Who was that you had to meet?"

"I don't know," he said.

"I thought I recognised him, but it can't be," she said. "Well, they must be important for all this secrecy."

He said to himself, *Well, he would have been very important a long time ago but it can't be him; he's been dead for over forty years.*

New Cross London SE14 is a borough of Lewisham; possibly most important of all is its mill wall country. If you're a football fan, you'll know what that means; anyway, three men were working down there, two of them were northern lads. They were best friends as kids, and even though sometimes as you grow up, you drift in different directions, they were still close, that type of bond some men have with each other. They have great respect for each other. Tony is thirty-three, and Geoff is thirty-four; the third man is a sort of local, he's from the Isle of Dogs, Gillingham. His name is Colin, he's thirty-seven, but he is now living in the same town as the other two; these men are road workers who lay anti-skid surfacing.

Saturday, November 21, was a nice autumnal day; you only needed a jumper on. The lads were in the local council yard they work out of; it's where Flexline, their firm, sends the equipment, gear, and stuff they need to be able to work. Here is how they lay the anti-skid surface: Andy mixes to appoints in a barrel with a big long electric mixer. Once he's mixed it, he carries it to Colin, who is in charge of the gang and the jobs. Andy then pours out the appoxin onto the road, and then Colin spreads it out with a large wooden scraper. When he's spread it out, Geoff puts the stone on top (bags of grit, really). Geoff pours the stone on the appoxin and then spreads it out evenly with the same type of scraper as Colin uses.

Back at the council yard, the three lads were mulling around really; they didn't much work to do.

Colin said, "There's only enough stone to do 150 metres."

"That's not a lot," Geoff said.

"Are we working tonight?"

Colin said, "We'll see."

Tony's been mucking about, kicking cans about; he told Colin, "If I get this can over the fence, can we go home?"

Colin said, "You'll never do it."

"Well," Tony said, "do we have a bet then?"

"You can't do it," Colin said, "the fence must be twelve feet high."

"You've nowt to worry about then, have you?" Tony said.

"Don't bet him," Geoff said. "He'll do it."

"He can't, it's impossible."

"It's Tony, he will."

Colin said, "Why you wanna go home, Tony?"

He said, "We've been bumming around for weeks, not doing a lot. I can go home and get some loving with that lass I'm seeing."

Colin said, "You want us to go home just so you can . . ."

Tony butted in, "Yep. Do we have a bet?"

"You can't, it's impossible."

Tony put a soda can on the floor, looked at the fence, then looked back at the can, and kicked it. It just made it over the top, a hell of a kick anyway, but it just made it.

Geoff turned around and said, "Told you he'd do it."

Tony said, "So we going home then?"

"I din't bet," Colin said, laughing.

Tony said, "I did it."

"I din't bet you."

"Well, what are we going to do then?"

Colin said, "Let's go to the pub and talk about it."

Geoff said, "We're not working then?"

Colin said, "We'll have two pints and that's it."

Tony thinks, "We'll be in the pub at eleven, two pints, yes! We're not working. We won't only have two."

Geoff said, "I want to work, Colin."

"We will."

Tony said, "You always want to work."

"Not a bad thing, is it? Just cause you're so laid back and don't give a shit about ought."

"Bit harsh."

"True though, eh?"

The lads got into their work van; it had a crew cab, which means it has a bench seat behind the front seats. Tony always sat in the back; as they drove along, Tony leaned forward and said, "Hoss racing is on the telly, let's get a paper so I can have a bet and watch 'em."

Colin said, "What the fuck is 'hoss racing'? There's no such thing as an hoss."

"Yeah, there is, don't you know what an hoss is?"

"It's a fucking horse, you northern cunt."

"No need for that, shandy pants."

"Well, talk fucking properly, you cunt."

Geoff, cool as you like, turned to Colin and said, "I used to like a lass once, she had an hoss."

"Fuck sake, you northern twats, talk properly."

Unusually for Colin, he was a bit mad; it was not like him, he was normally laid back. He said, "Tony, just cause you lot down here put twenty r's in everything you say, like farrrrrrking hell, well, we drop our r's."

"Us northern boys chop words down, it's easier than making 'em longer like your mob do."

Colin's a bit mad now because the two of 'em were laughing their heads off.

When they arrived at the pub, Tony said, "Come on, son, let's have a pint."

"Get 'em in."

"Why fucking me?" Colin asked.

"You're our leader."

"Fucking cunts."

They went inside; they didn't go into the main bar, they went into the other side. It's only for night time, really; it's dark and dingy. They all sat on stools, and when the bar maid came through, Colin said, "Three lagers please."

"No, Coke for me," said Geoff.

"If we're working, we're working, Colin."

"I don't know, what do you think, Tony?"

"I don't care," Tony said.

"He never cares," said Geoff. "He's more laid back than you are, and that's saying something."

Tony said, "We've had two pints; if we have another, then I'm not working. You're our leader."

Colin said to the bar maid, "Right, then two pints of lager, love."

Tony said, "That's it, then I'm not working."

Colin turned to Geoff and asked, "Wanna Coke?"

"No, fuck that. If we're not working, then I'll have a pint."

Colin said, "Another pint please, love."

Geoff was not best pleased; he said to Tony, "You're a git, you are."

He replied, "Bloody hell, Burt [when they talk to each other, they call each other Burt], we've been down here a couple of months now, we get all the shit the other gangs don't want, we're not exactly coining it in. It's not worth us being down here, I'm fucking scrimping on digs money. I'm passed fucking caring, mate. Sorry and all."

"Yeah, I suppose you've a good point."

"I have. Let's get pissed, mate."

"Yeah, good idea."

Colin turned to Tony. "Would you have gone home then?"

He said, "Yeah, why not?"

"Cause it's not our weekend to go home, and it takes two and a half fucking hours."

"So what?"

"Why, is she that good a fuck?"

"Well, I must say I like it, and it's betta than being stuck down here doing fuck all."

Geoff chipped in, "He has a point there, Colin."

"Will you two moaning cunts give it a rest? You do me fucking head in."

Tony said, "I'm not moaning, I'm just saying."

Geoff said, "Well, I've seen her and I'd drive back to see her."

Tony said, "Let's leave this one alone now then, but let's just see what the day brings."

Meanwhile, back at Sandhurst, the major's wife was taking the dog for a walk. Sandhurst is a big place, plenty of room to walk a dog. There's some wooded areas too, as well as the living and shop areas, but as she was heading back home, her inquisitiveness got the better of her. She went back by the house where the guests were staying. She noticed it was a bit quiet, nobody about, so she walked up to the house. She walked down the side of the house and noticed a gap in the curtains of one of the bedrooms. She looked in and saw the old man in bed. She thought, "I know him." His name wouldn't come to her, though, but her mind was working overtime. She got her mobile phone out, pointed it at the man, and took a picture of him.

At this point, the old lady came outside and saw her. "Hello, can I help you?" she asked.

"I'm sorry, my dog came running over here. I don't know what got into her, she wouldn't behave. I'm sorry."

"No, it's okay."

"I'm the major's wife, pleased to meet you."

"I don't mean to be rude," the old lady said, "but I can't introduce myself."

"Oh, not a problem. I'll get off and give the dog a drink."

She walked away with the dog.

The old lady said good-bye, and the major's wife waved. She went home and filled the dog's bowl with water and placed it on the floor. At this point, the major came home.

"Hello darling," he said.

"Hello love," she answered.

"How has your day been, dear?"

"Oh, slow; just got back from walking the dog." She looked sheepish.

"What's the matter, dear?"

"Nothing."

"Yes, there is."

"Well," she said, "I met one of your guests today."

"You did what?"

"Well, it's the dog's fault."

"Don't give me that, you couldn't resist, could you?"

"Don't be mad, dear."

"Look dear, they're meant to have total privacy. Nobody is to go near them."

"I know, the dog just ran off."

"Okay, but I've got a bad feeling about this."

"Why?"

"I don't know, I just feel bad."

"Why, do you think they're on the run or something?"

"No, I think I recognised them."

"Me too."

"You did?"

"Yes."

"Who do you think they are?"

"It cannot be who I think it is."

"Yes, me too, it cannot be, but I sense danger."

"You do? Why? You've faced so much danger in the past; how can you think like this?"

"Well, if it is them, where have they been all this time, and how have they managed to keep it secret all these years?"

"I don't know, darling, but let's hope they don't stay too long."

"Tell me, though, is there anything else you want to tell me? I won't be mad, I promise."

"Well . . ."

"I knew it."

"Okay, you promised."

"I know."

"Go on."

"I took a picture on my phone; I'm sorry."

"Okay, darling, but please delete it."

"Okay, I will, I promise."

The colonel started to think he should ring someone for help, but he wasn't sure. He thought it over and decided to ring Fred. Fred is SAS, so Fred it is.

The colonel rang him.

"Hello Fred, it's me."

"Hello, long time."

"Yes it is."

"What do I owe the pleasure?"

"Well, I don't want to talk over the phone, could I meet you?"

"Yes when?"

"Is tomorrow okay?"

"Yes it is."

"How about Buck Palace?"

"Oh okay, I get it."

"Yes."

"It's serious then?"

"I'm not sure."

"Okay, 11.30 okay?"

"Yes, see you there."

"Bye."

"Good-bye."

At the same time, the colonel's wife was on the phone to her best friend.

"Hi Jenny, it's me."

"Hey you."

"What you up to tomorrow?"

"Nothing planned."

"Fancy meeting up?"

"Yes, love to."

"Okay, fancy Alberto's, then maybe a stroll round the park, then maybe grab an ice cream?"

"What about a stroll and a chat first to catch up on things a bit and walk an appetite up?"

"Okay, you love their puddings."

"Don't know what you mean."

They both start to laugh. "What about Buckingham Palace? I love the park there."

"Yer okay, see you tomorrow."

Back at the pub, the boys had been talking away for a couple of hours; they had a few pints by now, four or five. Geoff was okay now that the beer had kicked in.

It was about three o'clock in the afternoon; Tony said, "It's a bit dark and dreary in here, let's go through to the other side, there's a few in there."

"Okay Burt."

"You fancy it Burt?"

"Yer, why not Burt?"

"Come on then."

They go through to the other side; it's quite full. For Geoff and Tony, it's the time of day when they come; it's busy, they're a bit quiet and sheepish to start with. Let's face it, it's a city pub, they're country bumpkins, better to be quiet till you get settled in and see how the land lies.

Colin went to the bar and ordered the drinks. One looked at him and said, "Okay, fella, I've seen you coming and going from here."

"Yer mate. I'm okay, thanks; yer, we stay up the road in one of Paddy's flats, we go upstairs for our tea."

"I thought you were from round here."

"Well, I was, I'm from Isle of Dogs, I moved up north, them two are northern twats."

"Well, let's not hold it against them, eh?" They both laughed.

He introduced himself to them.

"Nice to meet you boys."

"You too."

"Do you play pool?"

"Yer, we both do."

"One of you fancy a go?"

"Yer, okay."

They walked over to the table; the bloke said, "I'll pay, I asked you to play." He asked Geoff, "Heads or tails?"

"Tails never fails."

"Fucking did this time."

"Oh well.

"Is there a bookies round here, mate?" Tony asked.

"Yer, out the door, turn right."

"What, and just keep going?" he laughed.

"No, about 200 yards, can't miss it."

An old man said, "Yer, he's telling you right, youngen."

"Thank you."

"It's okay."

Tony went out to put a bet on.

"So what's your story?"

"Story?"

"Yer married? Single?"

"No, just live with a lass."

"Kids?"

"No."

"What about your gambling man?"

"Well, his wife left him for another man. He's got two kids."

"Fucking hell, that's rough."

"Yer, but two weeks after that, his mum had a brain haemorrhage."

"Fuck, how is she?"

"Not good, paralysed from the neck down."

"Fucking hell."

"Yer but he's a survivor, tough cookie him."

"Oh yer?"

"No, not like that, he don't like fighting but don't get him mad."

"No intention. It must be rough on him day by day."

"Yer, it's the kids, he misses them. He'll ring 'em later without fail."

"Fair play to him."

"Mind you, he's seeing a right sexy piece."

"Oh yer? Tell me more."

"She's only twenty-one, blonde, lovely figure, lovely looking."

"Good luck to him."

"Well, I think she has helped by coming on the scene. But he'd survive anyway."

"Look, don't . . ."

"You don't have to say anything, I won't."

"So what about our local lad?"

"He's same as me, just lives with his girlfriend."

"Nice."

As the two were playing, a few people put money on the table.

Tony returned.

"Okay Burt?"

"Yer Burt, you?"

"Yer winners?"

"Don't know, you never know."

"Will it be on the telly?"

"Yer, it normally is, I'll ask."

"Thanks."

"What bet you had, Burt?"

"Round robin each way."

"What's that?"

"Three horses, don't have to win, can just get placed, nice if they win though."

An old man sat down and said, "Good bet that, youngen."

"Thanks, do you follow 'em?"

"Yer."

"Had a bet?"

"Yer, a Union Jack."

"Never done one of them."

"Well, you can have a few horses for a few quid, if they all come in, it can make you a nice few quid."

"Nice one, good luck."

"You too sonny."

"Burt, you want another?"

"Yer, who's round is it?"

"Burt get 'em in."

"I'm playing pool."

"Priorities, Burt."

"Just cause you're a beer pig."

"No I'm not."

"Yes you are."

"No."

"You can drink fucking more than me."

"That's not really a good thing, is it?"

"I din't say it was."

"Well, I'm single, I get out more than you."

"No you've always been able to."

"Okay shut up get 'em in."

"Anyway I drink to forget."

"Forget what?"

"Don't know, can't remember, ha ha."

Everybody laughed.

"You're a twat Burt."

Tony sat down at a table to watch horse racing. Colin joined him.

"How you doing Burt?"

"Okay Burt, how are you?"

"Yer sound."

The two lads sat there talking about one thing and another, and then the horse racing finished.

And before you know it, it was about half seven.

"Bloody hell, Burt, look at the time."

"I know, it's flown."

"I'm just off to see if bookies is still open."

"Did they win?"

"No, they all got placed though."

"Is that loads?" Burt shouted.

"No Burt, but it will be a free day; that'll do me."

The old man said, "Well done, youngen."

He left and then came back.

"Bloody hell, more than I thought."

"Good get beer in then Burt."

"Okay."

They started playing pool between themselves and with the locals, having a good laugh and a good time.

It got to about ten o'clock; Colin said, "I'm pissed, I'm off."

"You can't, Burt, we're just getting going."

"I am, you fucking animal."

"I'll come with you, Burt."

"Fuck sake, it's only ten."

"We've been here since eleven."

"It was after eleven."

"Not by fucking much."

"I'm pissed, I'm off."

They both left.

Tony stayed there until twelve; he was well drunk by then and set off for the digs.

Sunday morning arrived; the lads were all well drunk the night before.

But slowly they started to wake up; Colin and Geoff woke virtually at the same time.

"Fuck me, Burt, are you rough?"

"Fuck yer, Burt."

Tony woke up and looked over at Colin.

"Fuck sake, you okay?"

"Well, I've felt betta."

"No, what the fuck did you do last night?"

"Nought."

"Well I think you're fucking dying."

Tony got out of bed and went to look in the mirror.

"Arrgh, I'm fucking orange."

"I'm gonna fucking die."

Geoff was pissing himself laughing.

"Fuck sake, Burt, it's not that funny."

Geoff bent down at the side of Tony's bed.

"I think this might be the cause of your illness, Burt," and he picked up a Chinese food carton.

"Fuck me, Burt, what did you have?"

"Don't know, let me think."

"Sweet and sour spare ribs, by any chance?"

Tony burst out laughing. "Fuck sake, shit myself, Burt."

"You daft bastard."

They all just died laughing.

"Fuck sake, Burt, did you eat 'em or did you just rub yourself down with 'em?"

"Yer Burt, looks like you enjoyed 'em."

"If only I could remember; don't remember anything."

"Good day though."

"You would say that."

"Why?"

"Look at you."

"These days don't happen too often; make the most of 'em."

"Looks like you did."

"Ace."

"What we doing, are we working?"

"Don't know, Burt."

"Okay, well, I'm off for a shower, then its coffee, then you decide, Burt."

"Yer."

So off toddled Tony for a shower.

"So are we working?"

"Don't think so, but don't tell him that."

"Okay." They both laughed.

Meanwhile across town at Sandhurst, the colonel's wife was waking up; she felt guilty at what she had done. She knew she had upset her husband a bit. Even though she knew he was kind and understanding, she still felt bad, but she was also feeling horny and sexy. She looked over at her husband asleep; she slowly slid down under the bed sheets. She took his penis in her hand and slowly moved her hand up, masturbating it gently, and then she put it in her mouth. She pulled his foreskin back to expose the tip of his penis, and then she rolled her tongue over the tip of his penis. He started to moan and move around; she rolled her tongue over the tip of his penis more and more. She slowly moved her hand up and down now as well; he was moaning, now really moaning. She started to use her head now, up and down, up and down, faster and faster, she could sense he was going to cum, faster and faster, up and down, up and down, then it came, his warm cum, she let it shoot down the back of her throat. She let a slight sigh of enjoyment out herself; she took it all and made sure she got every drop. By now he grabbed her hair and sat bolt upright.

"That's the best alarm call in the world."

"You like?"

"Hell yes."

"Good."

"You God damn are."

She gave him a cheeky grin.

"I'm off in the shower."

"Okay."

He lay there with a glowing smile on his face; what man wouldn't?
He heard the shower running; he started to think, imagining his wife,
naked, nice full breasts, hourglass figure, with a partly shaved pussy,
just a landing strip; he loved it. He started to get aroused; he's got a
decent size penis, his wife liked it, not too long, but it's the girth she
liked; she said it hits all her g-spots when inside her.

He thought, *Sod it, I'm going to try my luck*. He walked in.

"Hey sexy, want your back washed?"

"Why not, honey?"

He's very erect again; he got in behind her. She passed him the
soap; he started to lather her back and massage her shoulders. She liked
that; he slowly moved down her body to her bum cheeks.

"That's nice, dear."

"You like?"

"Yes, oh yes."

Then he moved back a bit and rubbed his penis in the crack of her bum.

"Ooohhh."

"Nice dear?"

"Yes."

She reached back round and grabbed his penis, rubbing it up and down, teasing him with her bum hole.

"You sexy baby."

He grabbed her breasts and soaped them; he tweaked her nipples and pinched them.

"Yes."

"Yes?"

"Ooohhh yes."

She wanted his penis in her now; she pushed back onto it. He grabbed his penis and slowly pushed it in, not too gently but not too hard. He got it all inside and shoved himself towards her.

"Ooohhh yes, honey."

"You like my cock in you, sexy baby?"

"Yes, dear, yes."

"I like my cock in your arse, sexy, do you?"

"Yes yes yes."

She turned to the wall, pushed towards him, and then just shoved towards him, slowly and firm, just so she can adjust to it being in there.

"Yes baby."

He grabbed her hips and changed the rhythm from slow and gentle to fast and hard, long, fast, hard pumps now.

"Yes yes, go on, please, harder, harder, go on."

He really gave it to her, he gave it all he had, he was really trying to perform. "I'm coming!" he shouted.

"No, not, yet hold, hold on, please hold on, God, yes, harder, faster. I'm coming too soon, please wait, fuck me!"

He gave all he had but he was struggling not to cum, luckily for him . . .

"I'mcoming!I'mcoming,yes,yes,ooohhhyyeesss,aaaaarrrrggghhhhh yyyeeessssss!"

He couldn't believe his luck; both their knees buckled. He was still inside, still cuming a bit, she was too. He grabbed her close to him, he kissed her neck; they stayed in each other's arms a few minutes, enjoying the moment.

"Well, sexy baby, that's what I call a Sunday morning."

"Welllll yes, like the old days, when I never knew when I'd see you again."

"Well, I think I could go back to them days for more like this."

"No dear, I've done my worrying, not knowing if you're coming home; we will just have to try and have more times like this."

"Hell yes, sexy baby."

"Well, I'll get out now and let you shower."

He kissed her and left, going back to the bedroom. He flicked on the telly, and then he spotted her phone. He couldn't help it, he picked it up and looked at the pictures, and sure enough, there's a photo of the old man in bed.

Bloody hell, he thought, *I'll delete it.* But first he sends it to his phone, and then he deleted it from his wife's. Then they both went through the motions of getting ready.

Meanwhile, back across town the boys all had a shower and made their way down to the council yard.

"So here we are again in this poxy yard and still no stuff."

"There should be a lorry here tomorrow."

"Yer but what time?"

"I don't know."

"Well, why don't we go home for the day? We'll be home for dinner pub opening time; might get a shag later."

"Is that all you think about—beer and sex?"

"No, don't be daft—Everton F.C. as well."

"Yer he does think of them too."

"Loves 'em."

"Fuck sake, don't stick up for him."

"He always does, always has done."

"Well, if I'd known what you were like . . ."

"Don't be like that, I'm the only one in the firm that likes mixing; you're lucky you found me."

"I' d rather have found a stray dog."

"I like that, funny."

"Well, you as good as did."

"No, you found him when I was, I know someone, you said."

"Yer and I did."

"And here I am, da da."

They all started to laugh.

"Fuck sake, what am I gonna do with you two northern bumpkins?"

"That's a new name, Burt; never been called that, have you?"

"No."

"Look, shut the fuck up. I don't fancy going home."

"Okay."

"Well., I'm going to go watch Cas, if that's okay, Burt."

"Yer, take the lorry."

"You're gonna travel all that way to watch Castleford?"

"Yer, why not? You would Everton, wouldn't you?"

"Well, yer but that's football."

"It's Everton, the world's greatest football team."

"Well, I'm going. I'll be back early morning, Burt."

"Okay."

"You want a lift home? I'll drop you off home on the way."

"No, I'll stop with this southern shandy drinking git."

Geoff just smiled at Tony.

"Yer, yer, I can't leave him on his own."

"Don't stop on my account."

"Shut up."

"What if I put the coke can over the fence again?"

"No. Fancy a trip to Buckingham Palace?"

"What can we do there?"

"Well, we could have a look at the palace, might see the changing of the guard."

"Whoopee."

"Sarky cunt, there's a big park, we could walk up the mall, there's hot dog and ice cream sellers."

"Whoopee."

"There's always loads of lovely women walking round."

"Well, changing the guard, what we waiting for? Sound's brilliant."

"Should have just mentioned the women first, Burt, and saved yourself time."

"Yer, he's a bugger," he said, laughing.

"Never change."

"Right, Burt, I'm off."

"Okay, Burt, see you tomorrow."

Geoff walked off and got in the lorry; the other two walked towards the van and got in. Colin always drove the van, especially in London, as he knew his way around.

Geoff knew his way home; he headed off to pick up the M11.

Geoff and Colin drove along, not talking much; they're not really talkative men. They drove along and then that song came on by Queen, "Bohemian Rhapsody," the one in *Wayne's World,* you know the one. I don't think either are particularly Queen fans, but just at that moment in the song, without looking at each other, they both gave it that head banging thing. They both gave it loads and did the *Wayne's World* thing to perfection. When they both stopped, they didn't say anything, they both just had smiles on their faces. Tony found it funny.

Meanwhile, back at Buck Palace, the colonel was waiting on the mall for Fred to arrive. He was on the far side of the road from the gardens, it's a lovely place. Behind him were some beautiful buildings of past kings and queens, mostly Georgian and Victorian, massive, tall, wide, proud buildings. The mall road runs along Buckingham Palace's western end to Admiralty Arch and on to Trafalgar Square at its eastern end, where it crosses Spring Gardens. It is closed to traffic on Sundays, public holidays, and ceremonial occasions. The Queen Victoria Memorial is immediately before the gates of the palace.

The colonel was waiting patiently; he took a quick look at his watch. Just as he looked up, he heard, "Hello, Colonel. How are you, sir?"

"I'm fine; thank you for coming."

"It's okay, sir," Fred said. "What is this all about?"

"I'm not sure. I've just got a bad feeling about something."

"Well, sir, what can I do to help?"

The colonel took his phone out of his pocket and showed Fred the picture.

"Do you recognise the person in this picture?"

He took a good look and said, "No, not really."

"Think of someone who has been dead quite a long while, probably the last man in history it could be."

Fred took another long look.

"My God, I think . . ."

"Yes."

"It can't be. It just fucking can't be."

"Yes, that's what I thought."

"Where was it taken?"

"Summerhouse, my command."

"Christ, what's he doing there?"

"I think he's come there to die."

"Why? Why there here?"

"Don't know; it's quiet and well guarded."

"There is secrecy, I guess."

"I see what you mean about turning bad, sir."

"You do?"

"Well yes, if this got out, the world would go into shock."

"Yes, there's one or two superpowers."

"Hell yes, the implications could be anything."

"Well yes, there's been decades of who and why."

"That's to put it mildly; there's been theory on theory."

"Why here, sir? Why would he think it would be safe here?"

"No idea."

"But someone must know he's here."

"This is dangerous, sir."

"Yes and he's not alone."

"Not his wife, she's been in public."

"No, think . . ."

"No, not . . ."

"Yes, her voice, got to be."

"My God sir, you're goin' to have to speak to 'em."

"They want total privacy."

"I bet they do."

"And what're you going to do if he does die?"

"Never thought about it."

"Well, you must, sir; somebody is going to have to. What, they going to bury him in the garden or the bushes?"

"Sir, I will help you now that you saved my life. I respect you even if you hadn't . . ."

"We're going to have to visit them; it will have to be at night I think."

Just at that moment, the colonel saw his wife walking on the other side of the road; he was just about to shout to her when Fred interrupted him.

"No sir, don't."

"Yes, okay."

The colonel's wife spotted her friend, in fact, they spotted each other and waved. They walked towards each other, embraced, and kissed each other on the cheek.

"Shall we go sit and have a chat?"

"Yes let's; shall we grab a coffee?"

"Yes, I'd love one."

They walked over and ordered.

"I'll get this."

"Thank you."

They got their drinks and walked over to a bench and sat down for a chat.

Just at this time, the two lads turned up; they've come through the arch and parked half on, half off the path.

"You can't park here."

"Yes, I can jump in back, we'll stick some signs and cones out."

"Okay."

Tony jumped in back and passed a couple of signs down. Colin took the big one and put it on the other side of the arch. Tony got a small sign, put it near the arch, and then placed cones from it to the back of the van.

Just as the boys were doing this, a thundering, booming, ear-numbing noise came from the park. Tony ducked down in total shock at the side of the van; he thought it might have been a gas explosion.

He shouted to Colin, "Burt you okay?"

"Yer, what the fuck was that?"

"Don't know; stay down."

"No, I'm coming over."

Colin came out from the back of the arch; he stooped forward and ran to the side of the van.

"Fuck me, I shit myself."

"Yer, me too."

Over the other side of the road, the colonel and Fred had dived to the ground; they were both lying down. They both knew it was a bomb because of the noise, but they also saw grass, mud, and bits of tree flying through the air.

"Terrorists?"

"Don't know, sir; let's take our time and try to play it safe."

The colonel looked over to the bench.

"My wife doesn't look to be moving. She . . ."

"No sir, leave her; you must. We need to see what's happening."

"For God's sake, I've got to go to her."

"Okay sir, but be careful."

"I will."

The colonel spotted the van and moved towards it and the boys.

"Hello."

"'er, hello."

"I'm army."

"Do you know what's happening?"

"No, stay down."

"Not a problem."

He ran over to his wife; he went up to the bench and called her name, but there was no answer. He moved over to her and put his hand on her shoulder; she just fell over to one side. He realized both women had their throats cut; the colonel just looked on in shock and horror.

"Colonel?"

"They're dead."

"Sorry sir." He knew.

"They've had their throats cut."

Just at that point, a shot rang out and the side of the colonel's head exploded.

Fred just looked on, stunned. He let out a big sigh. "What the hell is going on?"

The two lads saw this and looked at each other.

"Fucking hell, what the hell is happening?"

"Let's not stop to find out."

"What, move?"

"Yer, get in the van and fuck off."

"Pheww, that's dodgy."

"I think staying is too, it's either or . . ."

"Yer, true."

Fred saw the two lads and went over to them.

"You two, stop here."

"Why?"

"Just stay here till I find out what is going on."

"What's going on? What's going on? Bombs, bullets, and people fucking dying, that's what's going on."

"I know, stay calm."

"Calm?"

"Yes please."

"Well, he said please."

"Oh well, that makes it okay. He said please."

Fred got his phone out and pressed 1 on speed dial.

"Oscar 1 here."

"This is Oscar 2."

"Get the team to Buck Palace now."

"Okay, over and out."

The dust, the grass, the bark, everything had settled now, except for the people screaming, some with just cuts and bruises, some with far worse. One man was lying on the floor with one leg missing from the knee down; one woman was holding her baby, screaming for help, but sadly her baby was dead.

The two lads looked at each other and then at Fred.

"We better do something to help."

"You looking at me?"

"Yer, you can look at the injured."

"Yer okay."

"I'm not."

"Why?"

"Can't; don't do blood and guts and especially people's misery."

"I understand."

"You do? No speech?"

"No."

"Look, lads, cops will be here soon," Fred said. "You might as well leg it."

"Why? We done nothing."

"I know but you will be here for hours, having to give evidence; they may even take you away."

"Okay, if that's what you think. Burt, let's get the signs in."

"Okay, Burt, good idea."

At that moment, Fred ran off to help; you could hear the sirens in the distance.

"Quick, hurry!"

The lads ran around double quick, and they drove off in a state of shock.

Fred went over to the colonel, bent beside his body, and took his head in his hands. It was not a pretty sight, only a man used to it could stand it. The bullet had gone in on the right side of his head, came out the left side, and blew most of that side of his skull away. Fred looked over to where the colonel's wife lay; her throat was cut, and she was covered in blood.

"What the hell is going on here?" Fred said, speaking to the lifeless body. "What did you get into?"

Then he thought, *Why am I alive? Why not take me out too? Maybe they will in time.*

The sirens were close now, very close. Fred moved away from the scene and picked up his phone.

"Oscar 2, where are you?"

"ETA five minutes."

"Okay, Oscar 2, this place will be swarming in a minute; land near the Victoria Memorial, do you know it?"

"Roger that, we do."

"Good, straight over and guard the palace; I will meet up there."

"Okay sir."

As he put the phone down, he could hear the faint sound of a helicopter. He started to walk towards the palace; two guards were kneeling on either side of the gate; the guard inside was doing the same.

"Halt! Stop right there."

"It's okay, I'm army."

"Sir, please."

"Okay, son, but my men are on the way; can you hear them?"

"Yes sir, I can hear something, but I don't know who the hell they are or who you are. Can you identify yourself?"

"No."

"Why not?"

"Son, it's complicated, but technically, I don't exist."

"I understand, sir, but if you come any closer, I'll shoot you."

"Okay son, you're a good soldier, her majesty is lucky having you outside."

"No sir, just doing my duty."

"I know, son; if you had let me pass, I guess I should have shot you myself. But my men are going to land there if you don't let me; we'll have to tell them, okay? You would not want that."

"Is it a terrorist attack?"

"No son, I don't think so; there's a dear friend of mine dead up there, and his wife's dead too."

"Sorry to hear that, sir."

"Why was there an explosion?"

"It was a diversion to cover up the murders."

"Okay sir, I've radioed for reinforcements; when they get here, land your men."

"Okay soldier."

Fred passed up and down; he was annoyed. He was used to death and losing people (if you ever get used to it), but he was upset and mad about the colonel, and he wanted to find out why it happened.

The copter was overhead now and starting to make its descent.

"It's okay, soldier, keep your nerve; everything is cool."

The copter landed and four men got out.

"Right men, there's been an explosion but I don't think it's terrorists. Oscar 2, there's been three murders in the park near the arch about twenty paces in. Now I want to know what happened; there must be CCTV here."

"Yes sir, there is. I know where to look."

"Good man, take someone with you, we'll stay here. I think we're gonna have to talk to the authorities sometime. I'd like to get out without seeing them, but we may have to. Look men, this is not something we would get involved in normally, of course, but this is personal to me. I want to know what's going on and why, but it might lead to trouble from all directions, so if you want to leave and go back to base, I understand."

"Shut the fuck up; let's just get down to it."

"Four with me."

They ran off at the double.

"Okay, three, you know a bit about explosives. We will take a look at the bomb site."

"Yep."

The three moved off; meanwhile, the first group of men reached the CCTV control building, but how would they get in? They reached the front door, which was covered by cameras; they rang the bell and showed ID cards to the camera. The door opened, and they were met by two security guards and a man who introduced himself as the operation's manager.

"I know why you gentlemen are here."

"Okay sir, then you know what we want."

"Well, I'm going to have to break the rules and take the tape out before the shift is finished, but I've seen what has gone on, so I guess I better sort it out for you."

"Thank you sir; you should be okay."

"Okay, please come this way."

He led them to the control room and walked towards a man looking at a screen.

"Take the disc out, log it, then give it to me."

The man looked questioningly at him.

"Just do it; it's my call. I'll take the heat."

He pressed a button and out came a disc; he took it out and replaced it with another, then he moved over to a log book, looked at the clock, wrote down the time, and signed his name. The manager moved over and countersigned it.

"Come with me."

The manager led them to his office and sat down at his desk; in front of him was a laptop; he put the disc into the laptop.

"There you go; do you know what to do?"

"Yes sir."

"Okay, I'll grab a coffee; would you like one?"

"No thank you, no time really."

"I understand."

The two men sat down to view the tape; they fast forwarded it because they didn't have time to watch it all, then one of them spotted something. He pulled his phone out and speed dialled 1.

"Sir, where are you?"

"Checking the blast site."

"Be careful."

"Why?"

"Sir, the women had their throats cut the same time as the explosion."

"Okay, understood."

"Sir, this was no terror attack."

"What have you found?"

"Sir, this is state of the art."

"Yer?"

"Yer sir, this is radio controlled shit, no timer."

"I see, black op shit."

"Oh yes sir, no mistake, stuff like this can't be blocked by any other signal by chance, plus you would have to have a state-of-the-art signal finder and blocker."

"'erm?"

"Yes, and they used just enough explosive to cause a big distraction, but not too much death."

"Well, there's one or two out there not very well."

"Yes sir, but I'm sure it could have been worse."

"Okay, let's go see two and find out what he saw on the tape."

"Sir, I think this was done by friendlies."

"Friendlies? We will see about that."

"Sir?"

"Can one of you look in the colonel's pocket and get me his phone?"

"Yes sir, I'll do it."

He went over to the colonel's body, leaned over, and put his hand in his back pocket, and then the other, and then both his side pockets.

"Sir, I can't find it. It's not here."

"You sure?"

"Well, if it is, it's the smallest I've ever known."

"No it's not, cheeky sod."

He got his phone out and speed dialled again.

"You still at the control room?"

"Just about to leave."

"Go back and take a look again, thirty seconds before the colonel was shot, he was leaning up against a truck with two lads."

"Okay, I'll go back, we need to take another look, okay?"

"Yes okay."

They looked at the tape again.

"What do you see?"

"One second, sir, he's just gone over. He sees something upsetting, he's put something in one of their pockets."

"Shit, get back here ASAP."

"Okay."

"The other men were interested in that bit as well."

"What others?"

"I'm no expert but I'd say Yank spooks of some kind."

"Sir?"

"I heard; ASAP, man, get back here!"

Both sets of men set off to meet each other.

"Right men, right. The colonel, my old friend, was head man at Sandhurst; he had some guests. If I tell you who I think they are, you will think I'm crazy, but he and his wife are now dead, so those two lads have got his phone on them knowingly or not, now it looks like trouble ahead if we go after them, trouble we have no okay to do so, or I can walk away and leave those two lads to their fate and never try to find out if it is really them on the phone."

"Sir, we're inquisitive, and I know you are, so you know the answer any way."

"Yes?"

"Yes."

"Yes."

"Okay, then we go war mode; that means no 'sir,' SAS don't salute or anything. They were saying as cover their own idea as cover."

"Right, first thing, ring them lads."

The lads were now making their way through London to pick up the M11 and head home; in fact, just as they were about to get on the M11, they heard a ringing noise.

"Phone, Burt."

He looked at it. "No, not me."

"Well, it's not me, I ain't got one."

"Well, who the fuck is it then?" He leaned over to look at the phone and felt something. He reached into his back pocket.

"What the . . . , whose is this?"

"Hello?"

"Hello, listen carefully to me please."

"'er, okay."

"Who is it?"

"Don't know."

"Please listen, I'm a friend you've never met but you have to believe me; if you don't, you will die."

"Yer?"

"Yes, the phone you're on was a friend of mine's. You talked to him at the bomb blast just . . ."

"Just before he got his head blown off?"

"Yes, yes, please stay calm; there's a photo on there that some very nasty people want; take a look, I'll ring you back in one minute."

"He says there's a photo on here that some bad people want."

"Take a look."

"It's an old man, look!" He showed him.

"Yer, all that over an old man."

"He says we will die if we don't trust him."

"Well, I think we might be in trouble with someone."

"What do we do?"

"I don't know, I'm not James Bond." He looked back at him.

"Idiot."

"Why?"

"What's he got to do with it?"

"Well, this is spy type shit."

"Really? Well, you're more Austin Powers than yer Liz Hurley."

"Liz Hurley? No man."

"Yer, don't tell me you wouldn't."

"No but . . ."

"But what best tits I've ever seen, perfect, right shape, right size, she's gorgeous, and that voice makes me . . ."

"Yer, I get it, she's better than the blonde, Heather Graham."

"No, you'd give her one, yer, but she's no Liz, Liz is totally sexy."

"Well, neither are the one for me."

"Who is then?"

"J-Lo, Pene Cruz."

"You're like me, you like 'em dark."

"Yer, find 'em sexier than blondes."

"Me too, but I like Baby Spice, she is hot and sexy, but I tell you who I like, her out of Holby City."

"What, Tina Hobley?"

"No but . . ."

"Thingy then?"

"No, the heart surgeon bird; she is hot stuff."

"Her?"

"Yer, she got that 'I'd shag the arse off you if you're lucky enough for me to fancy you' thing going on."

"You're a lunatic."

Just then the phone rang again.

"Well, have you found the picture?"

"Yer, it's an old man."

"You don't recognise the person?"

"No, should I?"

"Well, hard to say."

He took a good long look.

"Hey, that can't be, can it?" He passed the phone over.

He took a good look.

"That can't be."

"I know it can't be."

"Well, if that's who we think it is, where has he been all this time?"

"Yes, well, that's why I'm ringing. You're in danger; where are you heading?"

"That's a question I can't answer."

"Come on, son."

"No, I'm out," he said and then hung up.

"They din't believe you."

"I'm not sure."

"We need transport with a sat nav in it."

Just at that minute, number three looked up; she was the latest top-of-the-line Range Rover; he thought, *That will do,* and takes a wander over.

He tapped on the window and it slowly went down. Behind the wheel was a man in a black suit and tie, he also wore an earpiece. He realized this could be one of the opposition, so to speak, so he punched him on the nose, dragged him out of the car, and then knocked him unconscious. He jumped behind the wheel and drove up next to the others.

"Quick, get in."

"Where?"

"Don't ask."

"How bad?"

"Well, I think it could be the not-so-friendlies."

"Oh my God."

"Never mind; well done now, has it a sat nav?"

"Do you think I would go to all this trouble for one without."

"No I guess not; punch dn229ju in it."

He did, and up popped a destination.

"Smart, I like that."

"What?"

"I don't think our lad on the phone is that daft; pretty cute."

"Cute enough not to get his head blown off."

"Well, who is?"

"Hopefully us."

They all chuckled a bit.

"Right, they might be able to track us on this, it must have some kind of GPS, yes?"

"Yer, probably."

"So do we dump it or gamble and plough on to where they're heading?"

At that, three pulled over, popped the bonnet, and took a look; he started pulling and tugging some wires, and then all of a sudden, he reappeared with something in his hand. He got back in the car and showed what was in his hand.

"They might struggle to see where we're going."

They all chuckled again.

"Inspired."

"Right, follow that arrow there."

They set off.

Meanwhile, back outside the palace, the man in the suit was slowly waking up; his two friends had found him. The leader was not happy.

"Where's our ride?"

"Lost it, sir."

"Fuck me, how?"

"Well, a man came over, then bang, never gave me a chance. I just didn't expect . . ."

"You didn't expect? You're God damned paid to expect."

"Yes, I didn't want to attract . . ."

"Yes, okay."

Meanwhile, back in the car:

"Okay, so you think you got the car off the not-so-friendlies?

"Yes."

"So why were they still around? They beat you to see the tape."

"Yes."

"So why were they still there? Why?"

"Well, they would have seen what we did."

"Yes, yes."

"They would need to find out who the two lads are."

"Yes, yes, that's it, they're trying to find out; so what?"

"The number plate on the truck; they'd have to start there."

He rang the lads.

"Hello?"

"Hello, friend."

"Look, we think they're trying to find you through the truck."

"We've just had a phone call from the head office; they said the police had rung and said we were in an accident."

"Clever bastards; look, did they give 'em your location?"

"Probably."

"Look, pull over somewhere, at least let them get in front, we will go to the house and stake it out. Hey, very clever how you put your post code in the conversation."

"Thank you, I'll tell Burt to pull over for a bit, what shall we do then?"

"Wait an hour, then set off for home. Before you get too close, ring this number, okay?"

"How do I know I can trust you? I've got two kids."

"Look son, you've no need to believe me, but please do."

"That man who came next to you, the man who died, was a friend of mine; he saved my life. I want these bastards."

"Okay, we'll think."

"Okay, son, take care."

"What do you think, do you think they will trust you?"

"I don't know, what would you do?" They all shrugged their shoulders.

Meanwhile, in the van:

"Well Burt, what we gonna do?"

"No idea."

"I know, if we stay on our own, I think we'll die, and if we don't, we will die."

"Yer well, like you said, we ain't James Bond."

"Yer, if only it was a movie, how the hell did we get into this?"

"No idea, but if it was a movie, might get to give Liz one, or I could have a brain injury."

"For God's sake, man, we might be murdered and you're banging on about."

"Well, nervous energy."

"Let's stop at these services."

"Yer, okay."

The boys pulled up in the services; they got out and walked towards the garage shop; meanwhile, back near Buck Palace:

"Right, we need to know about those two in the van."

"Did you get the number plate?"

"Yes sir."

"Right, find out who it's registered to."

"Okay."

"Right, then that man you let steal our wheels, who do you think he is?"

"SAS."

"Why?"

"I was watching them. They only said 'sir' to the older one, the one who met the colonel."

"Good spot, let you off him getting the better of you. This is bad, though if we have to take them on, you normally come second."

"Yes sir, but what do we do? Can we stop now?"

"Don't know, do we gamble on those two lads slinging the phone and keeping their gob shut?"

"Well, if they don't, there's gonna be one hell of a shit storm."

"I know, but can we really go round killing people in another country and get away with it?"

"Well, we've started, sir; the police are going to see that disc soon, sir. Do you think it will fool them? Do you think they will go for a terrorist attack?"

"Hell, I don't know; you can pilot a helicopter, can't you?"

"Yes sir."

"Right, get to our nearest air base. I'll get you clearance, then we will have to find those two."

"Then sir?"

"Well, betta to be safe than sorry; we will have to try pinning something on them if it goes tits up."

"Well, I agree, sir."

"Why did they have to come here? Why not just stay on that island?"

"They have their reason, sir; you know that they must have thought they would be safe there."

"Yer, I know, but if they'd stayed where they were, none of this would have happened; does it really matter where it happened? They can't let it be known who it is anyway."

"Yer, but if it was me, I'd like to choose where."

"Yer, but why here? Why? I don't understand."

"No, I can see your point, sir, but we're in too deep now, we gotta try to sort this out ASAP."

"Yer, you're right; betta get on your way. I'll radio you with instructions."

"Okay, sir."

Back at the service, the boys were having a Burger King, Tony was staring out the window.

"What you thinking about?"

"Liz Hurley."

"*Liz Hurley?*"

"Yer, why?"

"Why? We probably got killers on our tail who are going to kill us and you're thinking of a woman."

"Not just any woman."

"It doesn't matter what woman."

"Okay, calm down, talk normal; everyone is looking."

"Okay, can you just concentrate on how we will get out this?"

"We won't."

"Great, what an optimist."

"No, realist."

"What about them on the phone?"

"Don't know, how can I? They'll probably kill us."

"Fuck sake, go back to daydreaming over Liz."

"Well, what do you want me to say? I've got two kids and they're goin' to be fatherless just cause I went to Buck Palace for an ice cream."

"That's my fault, I guess."

"No, but I don't really want to die over something I don't know or give a shit about."

"What do you ever give a shit about? You're too laid back, you idiot."

"My kids, my kids, that's what I realize now, I don't do enough with 'em, I go home once a fortnight, go out Friday night, get hammered, pick 'em up Saturday morning, go home and mong on the settee all day, then take 'em home Sunday morning so I can go out again."

"Yer, well you're a good dad, they do know that, and deep down they understand and just wanna be with you."

"You think?"

"Yer, they know you love 'em."

"Thanks, so what can we do?"

"Don't know."

"Well, the phone, they know we got the phone, we could smash it."

"Yer, good."

"But will they believe we didn't look at the fella on the phone? He made me look, what about those he said would be after us? They wouldn't take that chance or believe we won't say anything."

"Oh yer God, that's true."

"I think we have to trust those on the phone or get guns and try to kill all those who come after us."

"Oh yer, like we can do that, I can't fire a gun."

"Nor me."

"So when they ring, I trust them then."

"Yer, no choice."

"True."

Back at Buck Pal, there were police cars, fire engines, and ambulances all over the place, it was sort of organised mayhem; the men were parked up watching and taking everything in, then the boss man worked out who was in charge and got out of his vehicle.

"Wait here."

He walked over to the officer in charge, pulled out a wallet, opened it, and showed his ID to the officer.

"Hello sir, what are you guys doing here?"

"Well, you know about us, we hear of everything, I can give you the number of a van I think has something to do with this."

"Thank you, what is your interest in this?"

"Well, let's not name names or mention a certain event not so long ago."

"Okay, point taken."

"Thank you for that."

"What's the van number?"

"nl08nro."

"Could you be so kind as to run a PNC check?"

"Yes sir I could, but I know what you said; if you find them, what are you going to do?"

"Look, we need to find them and question them, see what they're up to. That is all."

"Okay, I'll do it." He ran the check.

"It's registered to Flexline, a company in Lancashire."

"Where?"

"Chorley."

"Where the hell is that, son?"

"Between two and three hundred miles north of here."

"So they will be heading north then."

"Don't know, maybe, probably."

"Have you got the company's phone number?"

"Yes, here it is."

"Thank you."

"Right boys, let's saddle up and head north to Lancashire."

"Are we really?"

"No, we pretend, then I'll ring and try to find out were they live; they'll be heading home I guess." They set off to head north.

As soon as they were out of sight of the police, he was straight on the phone.

"Hello, Flexline, how may I help you?"

"Yes, good morning, I'm Sergeant Jones from the Metropolitan Police."

"Oh?"

"Don't worry, nothing too serious. We understand you have a couple of guys working down here."

"Yes, a few."

"Could you please tell me who would driving your van numbered nlo8nro?"

"Yes, that's a gang of three."

"Oh yes, let me get a pen and paper, okay, right, right, thank you, you've been very helpful."

"Okay, are they in any trouble?"

"No, we've been told they have hit another vehicle and not stopped. I'm sure we can sort it out with no fuss."

"Okay, bye."

"Thank you, bye, have a good day."

"That was too God damn easy, she just signed their death warrant."

"Dumb as English, just too polite."

"Yer, put dn229jp in the sat nav and you know the rest."

Back at the service station:

"Do you watch *Life on Mars*? It has that bird with the funny name."

"Is it Keely something?"

"For God's sake, not women again."

"Well, if I'm gonna get a bullet in me head, at least I will be thinking good things."

"True, but can't you concentrate and help us to both stay alive?"

"Yer okay, but she is fit as . . ."

"Yer, what about her who was in *Spooks* and then in that *Married Single*, the other, her eyes what eyes?"

"Okay, okay, now let's get goin' home; no more."

"Okay, just say you don't think they are sexy as fuck, cause if she gave those eyes, you're fucked, and the other one, she was in an episode the other night, and you could see her nipples through her shirt. She had eighties shit clothes on, and I'm sure you could see her nips all dark and yes knock one out stuff."

"I give up, I'm gonna die, I'm so scared I'm gonna die, and all I've got with me is you."

"What's wrong with me?"

"What's wrong with you? What's right with you?"

"Why?"

"Cause you're a fucking idiot."

"That's harsh."

"Oh really?"

"Yer."

"Why?"

"Cause we're gonna die and all you can do is babble on about women."

"Yer but come on then, what else do I do? Come on, tell me."

"Well, we need a plan, and all you do is go on about . . ."

"Yer, I know what you're saying, but what do I do? No, it's not about that, it's what do we do, cause we need to decide together."

"Yes, I agree, that's my point."

"Okay, let's think then; they must be professionals."

"Der, you don't say."

"Don't be sarky."

"Okay, sorry."

"I think the man on the phone was army."

"You think? Big call, that."

"I know, but I think he is, massive gut feeling."

"Why?"

"Been round army, gave me that impression."

"So if he rings, do we go with him?"

"Let's go to my place, if he's army, he will be there."

"Din't you realise, I gave him me post code in some answers."

"Oh yer, very good, very good indeed."

So the boys headed for their van, but the boy in the suit was on the phone again, then all of a sudden, a voice came over the radio in their car.

"This is Eagle 1, I'm in bound to your signal, over."

"Roger, Eagle 1, thank you. Track to our signal and hold overhead please and wait for instructions."

"Roger that, Eagle 1, out."

"What you got up there sir?"

"Oh, just some help if needed."

"Help if needed? He's got a Viper attack copter up there, most deadly in the world."

"Hell fire, sir, you gonna let that thing loose?"

"Well, he ain't here to whistle Dixie."

"Sir, are you declaring war on England?"

"No, just two people."

"Hell sir, that's a lot of firepower to take out to rednecks."

"Listen, if they go public, we're screwed. There's a whole lot of explaining to do by a lot of people, it would shake the world and bring disgrace on our country, a very famous family, my family, and hell knows what the Russians will say, maybe World War Three."

"Okay, understood, but it's gonna attract attention; you've got the park to explain."

"They'll have to pin it on me, there's no connection to me."

"Not yet, but there'll be an investigation."

"Deny everthing."

"Eagle 1, come in, Eagle 1."

"Eagle 1 here, receiving."

"You're looking for a white transit van, nl08nro; if you see this vehicle, proceed and take out with ultimate force, understood?"

"Ultimate force? Can you confirm the command, sir?"

"Yes, ultimate force."

Meanwhile, the army boys were still near Buck Palace.

"Right, men, let's think this through properly."

"Yes sir."

"What do we know? A bomb blast, two throats cut, and a head blown off by a sniper; not terrorist, agreed?"

"I would agree, sir."

"Yes sir."

"We agree, we think Yanks are in on this."

"Yes."

"Yes."

"Deffo."

"So my old mate is assassinated; on his phone is a picture of two people, it can't be, but as we speak, lads have said phone with picture on, me old mate was head man at Sandhurst, so it is a picture from there."

"Very possibly, sir."

"Yes, so what do we do next? Chase after these lads, because they are obviously in grave danger, or go to Sandhurst and investigate?"

"Both? Really, sir?"

"Yes, that's the problem."

"Yes sir, we should help them boys; really sir, none of this has anything to do with us or what we do. We should really just go home."

"Is that what you lads want to do?"

"No sir."

"No sir."

"No sir."

"Thank you."

"Right okay, three, you and me to Sandhurst; two, you travel north, try and help them lads. Be careful, watch out for them Yanks."

"I'll try and get you some help as well."

"Okay, sir, we're on our way."

At this moment, an unidentified man was about to knock on Tony's back door.

The man knocked on the door and then tried the handle; just as he did, blood and brains splattered over the wall. The man just slumped to the floor.

A voice came over the radio: "Contact down."

"What contact?"

"Contact sir."

"For God's sake, tell me you've not shot anyone."

"Target has been taken out, sir."

"What fucking target? Who told you to take anyone out?"

"Sorry sir, I misunderstood."

"He misunderstood? He's taken someone out? You've got a shit storm in the sky already. My God, we're gonna hang."

"Calm down, calm down."

"Has anyone seen the body?"

"Don't think so, sir."

"Well, try and clear the fucking mess up before someone does."

"Okay, sir."

"Who the fuck is that idiot?"

"He was meant to be keeping an eye on one of the houses those lads live at."

The shooter walked up and put a skeleton key in the lock; he opened the door and picked up the body. Just at that minute, a neighbour went to her car, midtwenties, very sexy lady.

When she saw the man, she said, "Hello, he's not in. I think he works away."

"Okay, thanks, I'm just checking something out for him."

"Okay, bye."

"Bye."

He thought, *How the hell did she miss the mess?* He giggled; she was a ginger and not blonde, even luckier. He dragged the body inside; there was a toilet straight to the right as you go in. He put him on the seat and shut the door. He went into the kitchen; found a bucket, some bleach, and a cloth; and went outside to clean the mess up.

Meanwhile, back at the palace, there was some thinking going on.

"Right lads, what do we do? Charge up north and grab these lads, see what they have to say, or do we stay here and try to find out what this is all about?"

"Well, if we stay, what happens to those two lads?"

"Well, we will have to get them some help."

"Yer, let's do that then."

"Okay." He took his phone out and rang a friend; he gave instructions on where to go and what to do.

"Right lads, that's sorted, let's think this through. The colonel was head of Sandhurst, do you think the people on the phone are there?"

"Probably, maybe."

"Where though?"

"Well, where would you put guests up?"

"The big summer house would be my guess."

"Yes, mine too."

"So all we have to do is get in there."

"Yer, how?"

"Why not just drive up front and show our passes?"

"Sir, we're SAS, our passes are for Hereford."

"I know, but if we go over the wall, we will probably meet gurkas."

"Yer, you don't wanna fuck with them little bastards unless you really have to."

"My point exactly; front gate?"

"Front gate."

They moved off, got in the vehicle, and headed for Sandhurst.

Meanwhile, the two lads headed for their van.

"Tell you what though, Burt, I gotta say Penelope Cruz and Eva Mendez, they're two shit hot Latino birds or what."

He didn't answer, he just laughed and shook his head.

"What?"

The lads were just about to get in their van when there was a massive explosion coming from the motorway.

They ran over; there was absolute carnage: there were cars and lorries blown up, on fire, you name it. People were screaming and shouting for help, some were walking round in a daze. The two lads just looked on in amazement, open mouthed. *What the hell?* they both thought.

"Look."

"What?"

"A van same as ours."

"Where?"

"There, look."

"How can you tell?"

"Look at it, cab might be half missing but . . ."

"What the hell did this then?"

Just then the helicopter flew overhead.

"That fucking thing."

"Oh shit."

They both realized the significance.

"Eagle 1, did you take out the target?"

"Roger that."

"Okay, we're heading north; track us, and stay close."

"Understood, over."

"Let's just say where these boys lived can't do any harm."

"Why sir?"

"Call it curiosity if you like."

"Okay, sir."

Back at services:

"Well, what do we do?"

"What?"

"Well, do we take our truck or hitch?"

"Good question."

"Well, they must think they've killed us."

"Yes, but will they take it for granted?"

"God knows but the copter has flown off up that way, look."

"Yer, good point, maybe if we stay behind that."

"Why not?"

Meanwhile, at Sandhurst, the men were at the gate; they pulled up and stopped to show their passes. The guards on the gate were just young soldiers in training.

"Hello gentlemen, can I see your passes please?"

"Yes certainly."

The soldier looked at the passes and looked back at him; he just raised his eyebrow and gave him a look.

"Okay, sir, that's fine."

"Thank you, young man; we know where we're going, okay? I don't expect anyone coming to meet me. That would make me very angry, okay, son?"

"'er, yes sir."

"Thank you."

They drove off.

"So boys, where do you think they will be staying?"

"Well sir, what about that big summer house thing over there?"

He mouthed "summer house thing" to himself with a puzzled look.

"You mean the summer house?"

"Yes."

"Well, why don't we have a look?"

They pulled up outside.

"Very quiet."

"Yes, surprisingly."

"Shall we go in?"

"Might as well."

"Hello gentlemen; can I help you?"

"Hello madam. I'm not sure about help."

"Why?"

"May I ask your name, please?"

"Christine."

"Stop the pretence, madam; you're Norma Jean Baker."

The other lads just looked at each other in total bewilderment.

One pointed. "She's . . . ?"

"Yes, Marilyn Monroe."

"Who died decades ago?"

"Yes, she was meant to have."

"Come on, you think I'm Marilyn Monroe?"

"Yes; can we go in please?"

The three others just stood there, open mouthed.

"Well, I don't think I should let you."

"Please, lady, I asked nicely. I will be going in."

"Okay, I see I have no choice; follow me."

"Thank you, but could you give me a minute? I need to make a phone call."

"Yes of course."

He moved away a few yards and took his phone out and dialled.

"Wow, what's going on?"

"Well, we've got your two chaps but things are a bit interesting here."

"I can hear; what happened? What's going on?"

"Well, we got to that address you gave us, there was a chap inside dead, their mate, I think, and a hostile, so we took the hostile out just as the lads turned up. We decided to walk to the pub and wait for our ride to get here; just as we got to the top of the bridge, a black 4x4 turned up and stopped a bit away from us, then that thing you can hear in the background turned up and unleashed merry hell on us. We were holed up in a dyke while that thing took potshots at us."

"Okay, anyone hurt?"

"No, just a few scratches."

"Well, I can hear you're a bit tied down, but I could do with those two lads down here."

"Yer okay, we need to take this thing out but it's not gonna be easy."

"Yer, okay, do your worst and get here please."

"Okay."

"Right lads; I know things are a bit hairy right now, but I need that fucking thing taken out; any ideas?"

"Yes skip, I have, but it won't be easy getting a shot at it."

"I know being in this dyke don't help, but at least it makes it hard for that thing."

"Yes skip, but we need to get a shot at the back of its engine."

"The back?"

"Yes, get as many rounds into back of that turbo; that will down it."

"Okay, so we need its attention round about where that hedge is then."

"Yer."

"Okay, baz ginger, you're the best two shots. Micky, me and you will go right, get out of this dyke, go behind the hedge, and head towards the other one, okay?"

"Yer got it, skip."

"Well, if it don't spot us and obliterate us, we'll lay down fire for this pair to take that thing out."

"You two got that?"

"Yes skip."

"Well, when we open up, be quick; we won't get much time. Once that thing homes in on us in open ground, we . . ."

"Yes skip, we know, we gotta do it fast."

"Okay, let's do it."

Back at Sandhurst:

"Everything okay?"

"No, got a few friends in a spot of bother."

"Oh, I see."

"What we gonna do here?"

"Well, if you've had a shock, you're in for another."

"You can't mean . . ."

"Yes."

"The picture on the phone, you actually think he's inside?"

"Well, if she can be here, why not him?"

"Well, I could see how she could be here, but him? Him? He was killed in front of the whole world, the whole world . . ."

"Well, obviously not."

"No, no, no, this cannot be real."

"Real enough for my friend and wife and several other innocent people to die."

"Well, that's true, but these two, where the hell have they been all this time?"

"Well, that's what we're gonna find out; come on."

"Thank you for waiting, madam. May we go inside now?"

"Yes, follow me."

They followed her inside; she led them to the bedroom. The old man was in bed with an oxygen mask on; the lady walked over to him.

"Are you comfortable, dear? We have a few guests."

"Yes I can see."

"Good afternoon, Mr. President."

"Good afternoon, young man."

"To what do we owe the pleasure of your visit?"

"Well sir, I think your son has been a naughty boy."

"His son?"

"Yes, his son."

"What has he done?"

"Well sir, he killed a friend of mine, his wife, and some innocent people."

"Oh, I see."

"Yes, and he trying to kill two young men too."

"Oh, I see."

"Well, he is doing this himself, not on my orders."

"I believe you, sir, but I'm going to wait and see if my friend can save them; they're currently fighting with an attack helicopter as we speak. I won't bring them here yet; would you tell us where you've been, what you're doing here, and how the hell you managed to fool the whole wide world about your death?"

"Okay, then, gentlemen, I'll put the kettle on. Who's for tea, who's for coffee?"

"No madam, allow me. I can't let Marilyn Monroe make me tea."

"Call me Norma please."

"Okay."

"I'll show you where everything is."

"Thank you."

Meanwhile, they managed to bring down the helicopter; it was close, very close, but they managed it, and they put a couple of rounds into the 4x4 to stop them from moving.

The phone rang at Sandhurst. "Hello?"

"It's done, our ride is just about to land, will be there in an hour at most."

"Okay, how are the boys?"

"In shock; it was bad for us never mind civies."

"Oh and yer, that lad in the house was one's best man."

"So not just work mates then?"

"No, he's very upset; they're both in a bit of shock, but he's okay."

"Yer, I can imagine; we'll just get 'em down here and talk to them."

"Yer, will do."

"Thanks, oh and top work."

"Thank you, and their friends will need a new ride."

"Okay, good stuff."

"Right lads, we have got the lads."

"Good stuff, well done."

"Everything okay?"

"Yer, they'll be here in an hour; now where's that tea?"

Just then, they returned from the kitchen.

"Tea anyone?"

"Any coffee?"

"Yer, there's a pot of both."

"I'll pour."

"This is surreal, being served tea by someone who died fifty years ago."

She giggled.

"Look, I don't want to talk about where you've been or how the hell . . . here, wait till them two lads get here and fill them in."

"What two lads?"

"The two lads your three stooges have been trying to kill."

"You're joking."

"No."

"My God, I'm sorry."

"Well, there's nothing to do with us but they're English, so it's our professional duty to keep them alive."

"Yes I understand; I'm sorry. I didn't know."

"Well, they caused a shit storm; it needs stopping now. I don't want to kill them but I will."

"I know, I understand."

"Well, them two lads din't start it, they were just in the wrong place at the wrong time."

"The colonel's wife, the silly cow."

"Was it her fault?"

"Sort of, yes, but she's paid the ultimate price, and so has her husband."

"My God, no."

"Yes, your men let a bomb off in the Palace Park."

"Palace?"

"Buckingham."

"My God, how bad?"

"Well, a few dead, a few injured bad enough, but the colonel's wife, they cut her and her friend's throats."

"My God!"

"You're shocked your men are capable of such a thing."

"Yes, I'm shocked, never thought, I'm sorry for all this."

"Yes okay, but why here and now?"

"Didn't want to be buried where I was."

"Okay, I understand; explain when the lads get here."

"Yes I will."

"I can't wait to hear your story. I guess you must have loved each other more than the world knew."

"That's the point, the world only suspected. No one really knew; well, that's not totally true, obviously some knew and a lot suspected, but Norma did something for me."

"Yer, that's obvious. She faked her own death, but she couldn't have done it alone."

"No she didn't, Hoover helped her. She got pregnant and was scared he would have her killed, so she went to him first and asked for his help. He came up with the plan, he took the photos, got one of his doctors to sign the death certificate, and put a John Doe in the coffin for the funeral."

"Brilliant, simple and gutsy."

"Yer I know, but when the pictures hit the papers, people believe their eyes, don't they?"

"Well, yes they do."

"He told her he'd do it, but obviously she would have to disappear forever."

"But she was probably the most famous woman on the planet at the time."

"Yes, but when you're dead, you suddenly only look like Marilyn Monroe; she used to get looks but as time went by, they faded."

"Yes, okay, I buy all that, and what's the worst that could happen if it all came out? A scandal or bad press for you and your wife. She's some lady to have done that for you."

"Oh yes, we love each other. Make no mistake, I loved Jackie though, I truly did, but not in the way I love Norma. It is so intense now and then. Pity I met Jackie first, but maybe a politician could not marry Norma Jean Baker, because of her film image, I mean, not her proper self."

"A bit before my time, but I've seen some on telly, the 'Happy Birthday' song."

"Oh yes, that's when the world started to speculate and the rumours started."

"Well, hell, she did seem to have the hots for you."

"God, she was so sexy, how could you resist?"

"Well, she was sexy on the telly."

"Telly?"

"TV, television."

"Oh, you mean the box."

"Yes, she's my sexy baby, you only get one of them in your life, and I intend to keep mine."

"Well, fair play to you; loads must have let them slip away."

"Oh yes, you might meet many a beautiful woman, but only one is your sexy baby; she has that something, that oomph."

"Well, I'm shocked you called her your sexy baby."

"Why, the bygone age or something?"

"Yes, suppose so. Well you went to extraordinary lengths to be together."

"Well, it has been worth it. I realize my life would not have been the same."

"Well, a true tale of love, sir."

"Yes, it has been."

"Yes, but how the hell did you pull it off? The whole world saw you assassinated."

"I know, but we'd heard there was going to be an attempt, so we thought we'd just go along."

"Yes but . . ."

"You mean was it me in the car?"

"Yes."

"Well, remember *Planet of the Apes*?"

"Yes Charlton Heston, wasn't it?"

"Yes."

"So a mask?"

"Yes."

"You've got to be joking."

"No, *Mission Impossible* too, if you remember."

"I've seen a few old episodes."

"Well, we thought, why not? If anyone found out, I would just have to go back to the office."

"Yes, then you just suffered an attempt on your life; brilliant."

"Yes, that simple."

"But who knew?"

"Not many; Hoover, of course, one or two of his agents, and obviously a makeup artist."

"But surely they must have wanted to tell the world?"

"Well, I just don't know. Hoover was a very persuasive man; you didn't mess with him, but he was also a true patriot. That's why he did it all."

"Really?"

"Oh yes."

"But once he got Norma out the way, why . . ."

"Why do it for me?"

"Yes."

"Because he was a true patriot; he thought I was a bad president, I would be bad for the country."

"Ha ha, really?"

"Yes, funny, I guess."

"Yes it is."

"So he was happy to do it to see you go?"

"Yes."

"Do you think he was behind the assassination plan?"

"No."

"Sure?"

"Yes, sure."

"So who do you think was?"

"No idea."

"Really?"

"Yes."

"Well, what about Nixon and all?"

"Yes, funny, I've read and watched all those programmes and books, whatever."

"I suppose Lee Harvey Oswald could have fired the bullet at me, the magic bullet theory. Not so magic for my stand-in that day."

"Yes, you killed a man, I suppose."

"Yes, I suppose I did. I led a lamb to the slaughter."

"True."

"Yes, I've lived with that all my life. I'm not proud of it."

"Well, really, what else could you do?"

"I don't know."

"If you hadn't, you'd have been killed."

"Yes, but an innocent man died that day."

"Yes, but not by your hand in any way."

"Didn't make it right though."

"Lee Harvey Oswald too."

"Yes, but you truly had nothing to do with that; he was always doomed."

"So for all these years, all the books, films, documentaries, and you've been alive all the time; it's got to be the ultimate practical joke."

"Yes, you could say that."

"So come on then, who do you think did it?"

"Oswald."

"Really?"

"Yes."

"Why?"

"Well, why else would he be there?"

"Why? What do you know?"

"He was a commie."

"Oh really?"

"Yes."

"You know what went on, don't you know the truth?"

"Well, I was told about the assassination attempt."

"By Hoover."

"Yes, he came to see me."

"He told me about Oswald, how he wanted to become a Soviet citizen. He was an outspoken supporter of Fidel Castro and his revolution in Cuba."

"I see, but wasn't Hoover always implicated in this?"

"Oh yes, he might have been involved."

"My God!"

"Yes, it was dark days back then, people trying to outmanoeuvre each other for power."

"Have you read Hunt's confession?"

"Never heard of it."

"Well, he implicates a lot of people, but they all led back to Bush and Nixon, really."

"Yes, I knew Nixon has always been a favourite for it."

"Yes, two people really wanted me dead more."

"Who?"

"Khrushchev. He thought I pushed him too far, showed him up to the world."

"Did you?"

"I suppose so, he thinks I was going to push the button, but I was waiting for him to first. I thought he was going to push first, turns out neither of us was going to, but he thought I was too dangerous, that I would go all the way, but nuclear war not really an option, never has been."

"The ultimate deterrent."

"I think he got in touch with Johnson; I think they did a deal."

"So how do Nixon and Bush come into it?"

"Well, Nixon really gained nothing in my death, even though he was ambitious; he may have just thought I was dangerous too. I think Watergate was something to it. I think they got rid of evidence."

"Will the truth ever come out?"

"I doubt it; in those days, maybe like today, you can bury things."

"I guess so."

"Well, like when I was shot, they took me straight to the hospital, but two suits turned up and just took my body, they said it was a presidential order by the new president, they made the doctor sign the death certificate and release the body."

"You were said to have massive head injuries."

"Yes, I did. John Connally was also shot that day; people forget that. He got it in the back, protecting me."

"What, from the famed second shooter?"

"I don't know, a second shooter could make sense, if Oswald was a patsy and they were framing him, or just to make sure the job got done, or a bit of both."

"Well, a second shooter would make sense, maybe they were setting him up, that's why Cobb came into it."

"Well, they're all said to have Mafia connections."

"I know, but why would the Mafia kill you?"

"I don't know, Khrushchev makes sense, Nixon and Bush had a hand in the Bay of Pigs, I think; they hated me and blamed me for that, that was a mess, lost some good men."

"Yes, but it's all claim against counterclaim, that was the game back then, and Hoover could have been involved but warned you."

"Yes, but how it was back then, the messenger was capable of shooting you."

"You got a good deal out of it all, really."

"Yes, I got to be with the love of my life and my son, and have a great life."

"Well, it's one of the world's greatest mysteries."

"Yes, here I am, you know what?"

"What?"

"The Nixon thing never sat right with me, it never has."

"Why not?"

"Well, what did he have to gain? Johnson still became president, maybe gonna turn out more popular than me; if I'm president, he's got more chance of beating me."

"You should know."

"Well yes, most of the implicated ones are CIA, but they took an oath to serve and protect me and the country, and that means everything to them."

"Well, that's an interesting point."

"You think so?"

"Yes, look at me, I might not technically exist but my job is to serve the queen and country."

"But would you kill the prime minister?"

"No way."

"Well, there you go, these men were patriots. I'm not saying they were angels, but kill the president? No, not for me."

"Well, you were there, you know me. I can understand your point of view."

"The Russians, yes, Oswald, yes; he had thin connections to some of them, but never proved."

"The Russians and Cubans hated me, for maybe good reason."

"Yes, they make sense: revenge."

"They may have made a deal with Johnson; who knows. Let's face it, he becomes president, that would tempt him surely."

"Well yes, that would tempt a lot of men, I suppose."

"You see what I mean about Nixon and Bush?"

"Yes, might have been bad apples but never wanted to spoil the barrel."

"Yes."

"But Nixon did end up as president; he might have just been clever, and a Bush got there too."

"I know, just smells wrong to me. Krushchev had good reason to want me dead, and there was a Cuban, I can't remember his name, I don't know why I can't, he was involved in the Bay of Pigs, Google the Bay of Pigs and the Cuban missile crisis, and you might agree with me."

"Yes, I might, but surely there was some Americans involved somewhere."

"Yes, there might have been. I was looking into gambling."

"Argh, that would get the Mafia involved."

"Yes, I agree, but if Bush and Nixon get connected to them, all their ambitions are over."

"Yes, I agree, but men do strange things sometimes."

"Yes, I agree, look at me."

They both chuckled.

Just then there was a faint sound of a helicopter.

"Here come the boys, I think it would be better if they don't meet you."

"Do you think so?"

"Yes, I think better to just let them go before your son turns up."

"Maybe, but don't you think they deserve an explanation?"

"Maybe, but ignorance can be bliss."

"Yes, it can, but they deserve to know, don't you think?"

"Yes, I agree, but you've kept your secret for so long now, why risk it? There's a hell of a lot of carnage to cover up."

"I'll make sure my son behaves himself."

"Well, I'm shocked he's acted like this."

"Well, he's not used to this; we've been hidden away for so long, maybe he just didn't know how to handle it all."

A second helicopter came into earshot.

"Well, here he comes. I think we better get inside, my boys can handle him."

———

He went back outside to watch them land.

"Right, get the boys inside, spread out, watch them land, and when they do, make them behave, okay?"

"Yes, understood."

The three went inside; the men took up their positions.

Inside, "Hello, I think you two have had a bad day."

They just stared.

"Bless them, they're in shock."

"Yes, they don't know what day it is or what the hell is going on."

"Give them a drink."

"Tea or coffee?"

"Tea please."

"'er, coffee please."

"Well, at least they can talk."

"Yep, that's something."

The boys sat down and drank.

"So the picture on the phone, it really is . . ."

"Is who?"

"John F. Kennedy."

"Yes, it's me."

"Oh, we're gonna die."

"No, no, I assure you."

"Really? Well, someone's been trying all day."

"It can't be, it just can't be."

"It is."

"It can't be."

"We're gonna die."

"Well, it is; why do you think they've been after you?"

The other helicopter landed, and the men had them under control.

"Hello, son."

"Son?"

"Yes."

"My God, this gets worse."

"Now then, son, I hear you've been a naughty boy."

"Just trying to protect you and Mum."

"What, by killing innocent people?"

"Well, what did you think they were gonna do, run to the papers or something? Who the hell would have believed them? They were just an old couple."

"But I just couldn't risk it."

"Risk what? If you hadn't killed me friend and his wife and those innocents, I would have told him to forget and tell his wife to behave and destroyed the phone; for God's sake, man."

"Yes but . . ."

"But what? Who the hell would have believed them, for God's sake?"

"Well, we're here now. What are you going to do? What about these two?"

"I just want to go home."

"Me too. I just want to see my kids, forget all this, and live a normal life."

"Well, it's your call, son. You gonna let us go and leave them alone?"

"Yes, he is."

"Yes, I think so too, son. I'm ashamed of you."

"Only to protect you, Mum."

"Oh son."

"Mum, I just didn't think."

"Well, you should start to think now and do a lot of it."

"Yes, but Mum . . ."

"No, son, killing people is not worth our secret. We're at the end of our lives. You should have come to us; you could have walked away and left us here to die in peace."

"But . . ."

"No, no buts. You could have gone back to where we've been all these years—back into hiding."

"Look, we want to get out of here; can I trust you not to go after these two lads?"

"Yes sir, you can trust me; we will go in the morning."

"Okay, we're going. Pleased to meet you, sir, and you, madam. What irony, to meet Marilyn Monroe and can't tell anyone."

She just smiled.

"Good-bye."

"Good-bye, ma'am."

"Come on, boys."

They left and went outside; he winked at one of the men. As they were walking away, he turned to look at the house. One of the men took a flare gun out and shot it into the open door; the flare flew inside, and there was a massive explosion. The whole house went up in flames, shattering glass and splintering wood.

"Why?"

"Would have come after us."

"No."

"Yes."

"He promised his mum."

"You believed him?"

"Yes."

"Well, I didn't. It's all over now anyway."

"My God."

"God has nothing to do with it."

"By the way, you got the phone?"

"Yes, I have."

"Thank you. This is what it's all been about?"

"Now get in the helicopter and go, and forget all this."

"Thank you."

"It's okay, now go."